For teachers everywhere – everyday superheroes.

This paperback edition first published in 2020 by Andersen Press Ltd.
First published in Great Britain in 2019 by Andersen Press Ltd.,
20 Vauxhall Bridge Road, London, SW1V 2SA, UK
Vijverlaan 48, 3062 HL Rotterdam, Nederland
Copyright © Robert Starling 2019.
The right of Robert Starling to be identified as the author
and illustrator of this work has been asserted by him in
accordance with the Copyright, Designs and Patents Act, 1988.
All rights reserved.
Printed and bound in China.
3 5 7 9 10 8 6 4
British Library Cataloguing in Publication Data available.
ISBN 978 1 78344 882 1

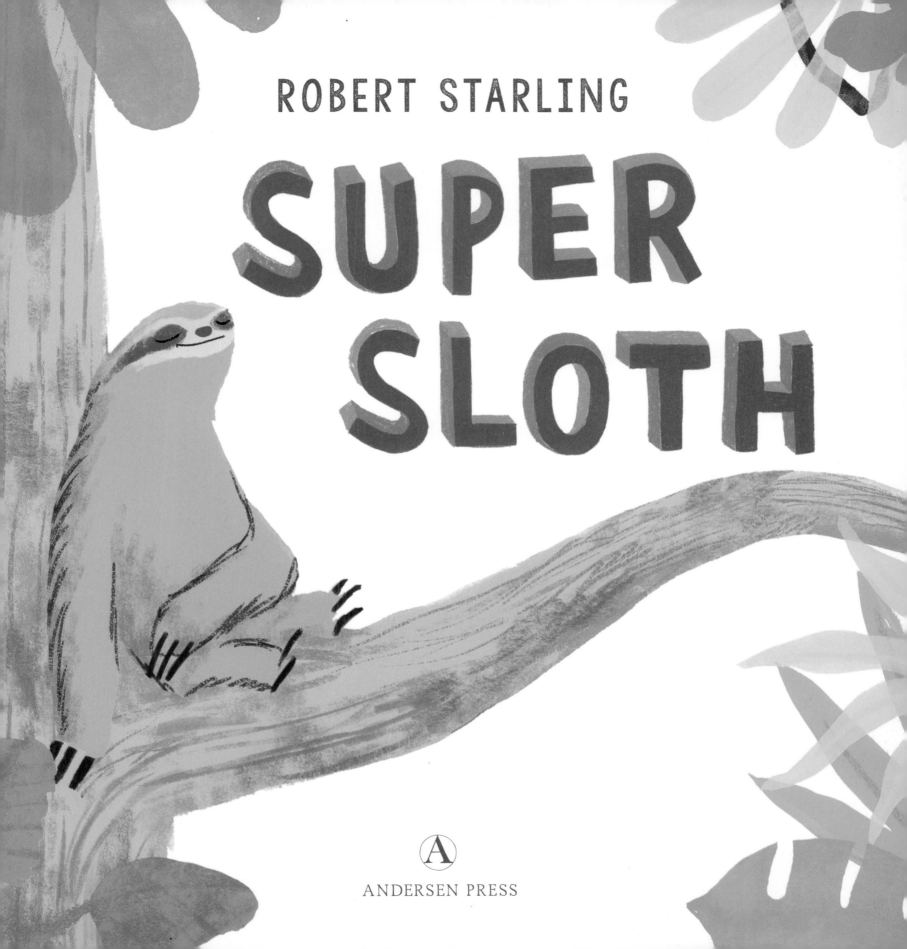

ROBERT STARLING

SUPER SLOTH

ANDERSEN PRESS

In an ordinary jungle, up an ordinary tree, on an ordinary branch, there lived a very ordinary sloth.

He hung out in the same place every day and nothing much ever happened.

Until, one day, it did.

"What a strange leaf,"
thought Sloth.

It had little pictures drawn all over it, and the pictures told a story.

Sloth read
it all day,
all night,

and all the
next day too.

It was
amazing!

Wow! What if
Sloth could be
a superhero?

All he needed was a costume like the one in the pictures.

He already had a mask.

And he quickly found a cape.

Then he was ready to go and save the day! (Very slowly.)

It wasn't long before
his super-sloth
ears picked up a
distant cry for help.

Help! Help!
Someone's stealing
my mangoes!

MWA HA HA HA HA
HAHA HA HA HA HA HA HA HA HA HA HAHA HA!

Sloth rushed over.

But by the time he got there,
it was too late.

"Botheration!"
said Sloth.

"It was that sneaky
Anteater!" cried Toucan.
"I don't have a single
mango left."

"Not to worry, Toucan," said Sloth. "I'll climb up
the highest tree, then I'll definitely spot the crook."

Eventually, something streaked across the forest floor.

"Now I'll catch that sneaky Anteater!" cried Sloth.

He stretched out his arms, spread his cape...

and launched himself from the tree.

"Bother," said Sloth. It didn't look this hard in the pictures.
"I guess I'm not meant to be a superhero after all."

The other animals
were just as glum.

"If we don't get our fruit back
from that greedy, guzzling
Anteater, we'll starve!"

"It's no good," said Bear. "We'll never get into his stronghold. He's got guards everywhere. Even his guards have guards!"

Bear had given Sloth an idea.
A sloth isn't fast.
A sloth can't fly.

But a sloth is very, very good
at moving slowly and looking
just like a bit of tree.

RIGHT!

And this sloth
was also very,
very angry.

Little by little, hour by hour, Sloth crept closer and closer...

Not the other animals,

not the guards,

... to Anteater's hideaway.

And nobody noticed him.

not the guards of the guards.

Not even Anteater.

And so it was that slow old
Sloth with his mossy fur...

He got right up next to Anteater...

and he said,

"Boo!"

WAAAAAAHAH!!!

Terrified, Anteater and all his guards ran away.

Sloth had done it – he'd got everyone's mangoes back!

From that day on, wherever there were animals in trouble,

whenever danger had to be faced,

brave Super Sloth would be there.

Eventually.